The Inspector Disappears

A Splinters and Boomer Mystery

THOMAS HARRISON MOORE

Chapter One

Mom answered the phone on that rainy September day in 1961. It was Grandaddy calling her. Mom loved it when her father called to talk to her. It was as if she was still a little girl again, and she outwardly showed a giddiness, just being able to spend time on the phone with her dad. He and Ree had been living in Clearwater, Florida for a few years now, so she and her children were not able to have contact with them, as they once had. Boomer and Splinters had been especially close to their grandmother,Ree, and missed her terribly, after her marriage to Grandaddy five years ago. His paternal grandmother had married his maternal grandfather, after his maternal grandmother had passed away. Splinters was happy for both Grandaddy and Ree, but Ree's departure to Florida had been a loss for Splinters. Before the move she had always been there as a support for him, as a sounding board for him.

Mom and Grandaddy must have talked for forty five minutes, when he asked her if one of the twins was available to talk with him. Splinters was sitting close to Mom, reading "Great Expectations" for English class. He was just fine for being distracted, as he was only halfway into the Dicken's novel, and it had been a long one thus far. Mom said goodbye to her father, and handed Splinters the phone. He said hello to his grandfather, and Grandaddy got right to the point. "Splinters, I want you and Boomer to get together with your other two friends in the next few days", he stated in a commanding voice. (His voice was always commanding) He was referring, of course to Norm and Jon, who were close friends, but who had also helped the twins unravel and solve the mystery of the disappearance of their friend, Vincie. Without their investigative skills, he and Boomer would never have solved the case. Granddaddy talked on: "Inspector Scharffenberg and I have been discussing a serious case. He will be arriving in Columbus within the week to see the four of you boys and to help him work on this case. If he discusses any facets of the case with you, listen to him and give him suggestions. But, do not in any way become involved in the case he is investigating. This is nothing for four teenagers to be a part of. Do you clearly understand me?" Splinters assured Grandaddy he did understand. But the wheels in Splinter's head were already turning to learn more about another mysterious case. Splinters talked to Ree for a few minutes, then said his goodbyes and hung-up the phone.

Mom smiled at Splinters. "Hmm", she said, "did that conversation have anything to do with my forty seventh birthday coming up next week?" Splinters smiled back, saying "One never knows, does one? I must return to my exciting Dickens novel". To share this news with his twin brother was the feeling of excitement- to tell Boomer, but also Norm and Jon. It was always interesting to spend time with Inspector Scharffenberg, but to have him discuss a new case with them was beyond excitement. A thrill of mystery was attached to the feeling.

Splinters knew he needed to have Boomer, aloneg with Norm and Jon, to plan a party next week for Mom's birthday, so as not to hurt her feelings. However the birthday planning would take fifteen minutes, then he would tell the other two boys the big news.

Splinters ran upstairs to let Boomer in on the news, then called Norm. Norm told him that he, Boomer, and Jon could come over to his house after dinner that night to play 45 rpm records in Norm's basement family room. Splinters then called his friend Jon. Jon was pleasantly surprised to hear from Splinters, as both boys had been busy with school work and had not had any time to get together. Jon agreed to be at Norm's house that night. Jon lived just across the street from Norm on West New England Avenue in Worthington, so his walk was a short one.

Chapter Two

Boomer and Splinters walked from their home at 291 Mc Coy Road to the Sielisch home. They were both full of wonder about the new case. As they approached the attractive colonial ranch home, suddenly two large persons ran into them! Splinters was sideswiped by a handsome and smiling Jon, who fully embraced Splinters and lifted him into the air with those strong swimmer arms. Boomer was hit hard by a tall chunky Norm with thick rimmed silver glasses and an evil grimace, who held and lifted him by large somewhat flabby arms. "I've got the weakling of the two of them", Jon snorted to Norm. Norm, in his usual wit, said, "Good, dear, I have the stupid one". All four boys began laughing. Splinters thought how he loved these two guys, as he was gently placed back on the driveway.

The boys merrily walked into the home and immediately headed for the basement. Mrs. Sielisch had left them cookies and milk. There was always delicious food in that home. Tonight it would be homemade peanut butter; last week it had been chocolate chip. Norm's mother was a wonderful cook and baker.

Splinters sipped his milk, telling the other three about Mom's birthday party. It would be a surprise, and Norm and Jon would decorate the twins' home, while Splinters, Boomer and Virginia Kay, the twins' younger sister, were at The Old Worthington Inn enjoying Mom's dinner. Splinters stared at both of his friends, could no longer wait and eagerly spilled the good news about the inspector's arrival in the next few days. Jon suggested they invite Vincie to join them, as it was a certainty the boys would meet Inspector Scharffenberg at Bernie's Drug Store, where the inspector would treat them to cherry and lime phosphate drinks. Bernies and the phosphate drinks had become quite a tradition for the boys, Vincie, and Inspector Scharffenberg.

Norm grabbed some of his 45 platters, put them on his RCA record player and began dancing around. Jon danced around him singing "Who Put the Bomp in the Bomp De Bomp", a popular hit by Barry Mann. Splinters sang the song; he had it memorized. He used his empty glass of milk as a microphone, while Jon yelled in his ear, "Who put the Bomp in the bomp de bomp de bomp, who put the ram in the rama lama ding dong". John put his warm arm around Splinter's waist as they sang. They were such a duo. The second song was Norm's second favorite song, "Hats Off to Larry" by Del Shannon. Norm's favorite song was third, Del Shannon's "Runaway" with the calliope sound in the background. All four of the boys sang those two songs and were quite the quartet. The fourth song was one only Norm loved, “Baby Sittin’ Boogie” by Buzz Clifford. It was one of those silly songs Splinters thought. That night the boys sang and danced to rock ‘n roll, forgot about school and about the mystery that was about to become a part of their lives.

Chapter Three

Mom's dinner was a success at The Old Worthington Inn. The family had eaten the delicious fried chicken and roast beef from the inn's "Harvest Table Buffet". But Mom was totally shocked, when she opened the living room door of their home to find Norm and Jon screaming "Happy Birthday". The night was fun with more rock 'n roll. Splinters and Boomer gave her two 45's by her then-favorite singer, Brenda Lee. One was "I Want to Be Wanted" and the other was "You Can Depend on Me". Norm rolled his eyes at these two sappy songs. Mom gave him a little slap on his cheeks. Both of them laughed.

Once the festivities were over, Dad, accompanied by the twins, drove the other two boys home. As Dad pulled into Jon's drive, Jon began to get out of the car, as it was still moving. Norm yelled, "Jon, write when you find work". It was such a funny remark, and all five of them laughed for a few minutes. Splinters wondered how Norm came up so quickly with such funny, but witty, jokes. Mom had once told Norm he should take over Johnny Carson's job as emcee of the late show, once he grew up, of course.

Later that night Jon called and asked Splinters if he had heard from Inspector Scharffenberg-Jon had not. Splinters told him that he had heard nothing from him. Jon said he was worried. Splinters told him he always worried, and that he would call Grandaddy to check if he had heard from him. After hanging up with Jon, Splinters made the call. Ree answered and was so glad the party had been a success. She then put Grandaddy on the line. When Splinters inquired if he had heard from the inspector, Grandaddy answered "negative". Sometimes he could be so much like Broderick Crawford, the lead actor on the series, "The Highway Patrol'. Grandaddy said he would make some inquiries the next morning by calling the Columbus Police Station. He still maintained some contacts, as he had been the police chief ten years ago.

That night Splinters, while trying to go to sleep, told Boomer that he was worried about the inspector. He was supposed to have shown up by the time of Mom's party. Splinters went to sleep with the words of the mushy songs of Brenda Lee in his head. He also tried to memorize translations for his first hour Monday morning Latin class with Mrs Drumm. "The Aeneid" was a great story of early Romans, but translating it to English could at times be a bit difficult.

Chapter Four

The next day did not bring good news. Apparently, Inspector Scharffenberg had left New York City by air four days ago, headed for Columbus. No one at the Columbus Police Station had seen him. Jon told Splinters the four boys meet the next day at 4:00 PM at Bernie's Drug Store to discuss the situation. Jon was also going to try to involve Vincie to help them. He had been a great help to them a few months ago, after his disappearance and the mystery involving the Nazi sympathizers, Henri Mordello and Lily Fontaine.

At 4:00 PM, the next day, the four boys sat in gloom at the far booth of the drug store. Jon and Splinters had their usual cherry phosphates, while the other three boys drank lime ones. Even Norm had no plan. The inspector had been seen boarding the plane by fellow officers, so he obviously had arrived at Port Columbus. There was also a sighting of him after he had boarded the plane by an airline stewardess. Jon said he was deeply worried. Splinters tried to comfort him by telling him the inspector would turn up and things would be fine. Jon put his arm around his best friend, saying nothing, but looking very sad. He got up and said he needed to walk home and think. Splinters asked him if he needed some company. Jon smiled, showing his perfect white teeth, saying "I would love it". The two boys left the other three. Splinters walked with Jon to his house. Finding a plan seemed impossible, as they had no leads. Jon asked Splinters if he would call Grandaddy from Jon's house. Perhaps the inspector had told Grandaddy some little thing that could become a significant lead. They were dead in the water with no clues in sight. Splinters agreed to the call.

The boys made the collect call to Clearwater, Florida. Grandaddy said he could talk, as Ree was in a back garden with her plants. Splinters told him that Inspector Scharffenberg had probably arrived in Columbus, but his whereabouts from that point were unknown. Splinters then asked Grandaddy to try to remember if the inspector had possibly said anything that could give them a lead. Granddaddy was not happy about Splinters and his friends becoming involved in any "monkey business" concerning Inspector Scharffenberg's assignment and possible disappearance. Grandaddy could not remember anything of significance. Jon asked if he could talk to him, and Splinters handed the phone to Jon. Jon asked Grandaddy if the inspector had mentioned any word or phrase. Anything, however small, could be a lead, but Grandaddy could give him no recollections. He did say he would keep thinking about the entire conversation with the inspector, and Jon told him anything he could remember could lead to a clue. Both boys were extremely worried and concluded the inspector must have disappeared after he had arrived in Columbus.

Jon called and invited Splinters to dinner at The Old Worthington Inn. But first they would each buy a 45 rpm record at The Music Box, just a few stores from the inn. Jon wanted to erase their worries, as the inspector might have gotten off the plane and immediately started working a piece of the case. Splinters told Jon not to spend money on him, but Jon said he was "Daddy Warbucks" from being a swimming instructor and lifeguard all summer. So Splinters agreed. He then called Mom to not expect him home until seven or eight. "Yes", he answered her, "I will do my homework by eight o'clock". He and Jon walked through the late September day up New England Avenue toward High Street. Neither knew what to do about the mystery, so they agreed to think and talk rock 'n roll.

Splinters loved the smell of The Music Box. The aroma was of hundred of albums, 45's, new and old. Splinters spun the 45 record carousel around, looking for a new song. He found the perfect record, "Will You Love Me Tomorrow" by The Shirelles. Then John picked "Dedicated to the One I Love" by the Shirelles. He gave Splinters one of those wonderful smiles. Splinters knew John thought of him as his partner, maybe even his brother. John paid for the records, and they walked over to The Old Worthington Inn. The inn had been built in 1835 as a private residence, three stories high and neo-classical colonial. They both ordered the fried chicken with mashed potatoes and lots of gravy and gobbled it down. The talk was music. Splinters told Jon The Shirelles were one of the newer groups he liked, as they were pop but also a bit of rhythm 'n blues. He felt the girl groups were going to start to be popular. He babbled on while Jon thought. Splinters knew he was thinking of Inspector Scharffenberg. As they left the inn Jon said he would walk home with Splinters, then turn back around and head for his home. He needed to think about things.

The boys arrived at the twins' home around 7:30. Jon wanted to tell Mom and Dad hello, so he walked into the living room of the recently built split level home, just a year old. The creek ran by the house, and the woods surrounded the home. It was a gorgeous setting, as it sat at the bottom of the ravine.

Mom saw Jon, smiled and said "Hi Handsome", let's see those perfect teeth". Jon gave her his smile. Mom told him he was better looking than Paul Newman. Virginia Kay ran up to him and told him he was HER boyfriend. He told her he was excited and was honored. She asked what honor meant. Splinters explained it meant being trustworthy, and she asked what trustworthy meant. Mom told her it meant "being good". Virginia Kay understood what good meant. Dad told Jon he would drive him home, but Jon told him he had to think about some things and would walk home. Splinters decided to walk with Jon to New England Avenue, and he told him to stop worrying. Jon was mostly silent as they walked, and upon parting, Jon hugged Splinters in a warm bear hug and apologized for being so quiet. Splinters headed for home and thought how much love he felt for Jon. How could one guy express it to another guy without both of them being homos, Splinters wondered. Jon had expressed his feelings to Splinters numerous times, but Splinters, as usual, felt the same feelings as Jon but could not express them openly and honestly.

Chapter Five

Fall arrived in Worthington with vivid splashes of color. The village appeared so quaint during this season. He began looking forward to Halloween and the holiday season. It was a time to try to forget the negative and stop worrying about the inspector.

But those feelings changed on Halloween day. Grandaddy called Mom to talk to her then asked for one of the boys. "Grim news" he told Splinters, "so prepare yourselves and look out for your sensitive friend Jon. Inspector's Scharffenberg's body was found yesterday in the Scioto River in downtown Columbus. You and Boomer must buck up and go in person to your two friends to give them the bad news". Splinters was shaken but told Grandaddy he would follow his orders. Boomer was equally upset as Splinters, but agreed they must walk over immediately to see Norm and Jon.

As the two boys walked through the crackling dead leaves along the sidewalks, Splinters thought about death and how it shocked and numbed the human brain of the living beings, who had to live with that loss. The feeling was overwhelmingly terrible. It was even worse to have to inform both Norm and

Jon of the news. As they approached Norm's house, Boomer said he would go alone to Norm to tell him, and that Splinters needed to be very strong and go tell Jon alone. Splinters agreed. This would not be an easy duty to perform.

Splinters knocked on the door of the ranch home across from Norm's similar ranch home. Jon's dad answered the door and gave Splinters a merry greeting. Splinters felt somewhat happy that at least Jon's father was in a good mood. He knocked on Jon's bedroom door, and Jon was pleasantly surprised to see him. He had been cleaning his room, straightening his model cars and his 45 rpm records. He noticed that Splinters had something serious to tell him and motioned Splinters to sit on his bed. He sat next to Splinters with a puzzled look. Splinters told Jon the awful news. At first he simply looked at Splinters, not comprehending what he had just heard. Then tears started welling up in his eyes, and he started sobbing. He reached for Splinters for support, but in grabbing Jon's arms, he also began to cry. It was a sad and ironic scene as "Crying" by Roy Orbison was playing on Jon's record player. Splinters did not know what else to do but hold Jon tight as he took deep breaths in between sobs. Splinters told him that Grandaddy had told them to buck up as best they could through this ordeal. Jon agreed, but he could not stop crying. Splinters started crying again, this time because he was so affected by Jon's open feelings.

All of a sudden, there was a knock at the bedroom door. It was a teary-eyed Norm and Boomer. Boomer closed the door then told the other two boys that Mom had called at Norm's house. She told Boomer that Grandaddy had called and wanted Jon to call him collect right away. Grandaddy only wanted to talk to Jon. Splinters knew that tough old man cared a great deal for this sensitive teenager, who tried to be so tough on the outside.

That news got Jon up, and he immediately ran into the hallway to make the call. The three boys could hear him saying "yes sir" three or four times, then "yes sir, I promise to buck up, and thank you, goodbye sir". Jon came back into the room, wiping his face. He said the call from Grandaddy made him feel stronger. He also said Grandaddy had remembered a curious thing Inspector Scharffenberg had told him in that phone call some weeks ago. The inspector, out of context, had told Grandaddy that at times he, the inspector, could be such a "klutz, kooky and klunky, all words with the letter 'k' ". Grandaddy had told Jon he had, previously, thought it had been a stupid remark, but now there could be significance to it. The only three "k's" he knew stood for "Ku Klux Klan". Jon told the boys he wondered if the remark was to alert them to something about the organization.

Norm told the boys, for raking the front and side yard that morning, his father had given him twenty dollars. “Since I am so rich now, the four of us are walking to Graceland Shopping Center, to buy four 45’s, one each, at Harmony House and to have four hamburger platters with milk shakes at Woolworth’s lunch counter. They would, on Halloween night, have their own little dance party in Norm’s family room basement. The other three boys started laughing, wiping their tear-stained faces. Norm did stipulate a condition, ‘No buying any of that country shit you three love”. That got them all laughing, as they started their long walk to Graceland. As they started walking Splinters and Jon sang Patsy Cline’s “I Fall to Pieces”, with Norm at one point chasing after Jon to stop his duet with Splinters. But, then Boomer sang it with Splinters, and Norm said he was reconsidering his offer. Suddenly there was silence.

On the walk along High Street they were again figuring plans to devise. They now had a lead. Splinters informed the others that due to black civil rights protests starting in the country, the Ku Klux Klan was again becoming more openly active. But none of them could remember any problems with the Klan in Columbus. Norm said it was back to the library to research.

In Harmony House the four boys made their careful purchases. Jon picked “I Like It Like That” by Chris Kenner. Splinters picked “A Little Bit of Soap” by The Jarmels. He loved to sing along to that song. Boomer picked “I Really Love You” by The Stereos. Norm’s choice was a fast rockin’ song, “Pretty Little Angel Eyes” by Curtis Lee. All of the songs were fast dance songs, but also great lyrics to sing.

The lunch at Woolworth’s became a little dramatic, when Jon on the end, facing west, threw a French fry into Norm’s shake, as Norm sat on the end, facing south. Boomer, who sat to the right of Norm, responded with a tiny piece of hamburger right into Jon’s shake. Splinters, facing west sitting next to Jon, attacked Boomer with a pickle into his shake. Jon then smeared catsup onto Splinter’s left cheek. They were laughing so loud and becoming so obnoxious, the waiter almost threw them out of the store. But it had been the perfect release for the grim news they all had to go through that day.

Halloween night was equally fun with dancing and being just silly. None of the boys were currently dating. Norm was no longer seeing Sandy. Jon and Penny had broken up for the third time. Splinter’s romantic nights with Sherry had ceased once school began, as had Boomer’s nights with Sally. Mrs. Sielisch had prepared cupcakes with orange frosting for the four boys. The hard day passed into the fun night.

Chapter Six

November passed with no progress on their research. The days became short and cold. That Thanksgiving Splinters and Boomer went with Mom, Dad and Virginia Kay to their aunt and uncle's home for dinner. Don and Lois had just built a new sprawling ranch home off Olentangy River Road on Meeklyn Drive, just south of Linworth. It was beautiful but a way too much room for them and their spoiled poodles, Chrissy and Penny.

As the family arrived, Lois told the boys to kiss Chrissy and Penny before they saw the new home. Splinters felt it was so "icky", as the twins were ordered to kiss them on the lips. Splinters pretended to, but spit a little on their lips as his lips got close, then stood up, smiling at Lois. She smiled back.

Lois had prepared a delicious dinner, and she was unusually not critical. Don said so little, and mostly answered questions. He was never overly engaging. Lois liked to talk, and she mentioned that the "negroes" in the country should stop protesting so much in the south. They now had rights. Splinters kept it to himself that she was so wrong! She further went on to proclaim, "that socialist President Kennedy was causing trouble, getting the negroes to think they had too many rights". She shook her head and lamented that "the smart Richard Nixon should have been elected." Splinters wanted to throw up-on her. She then mentioned something that caught the twin's attention. "The Ku Klux Klan" in Columbus is starting to receive attention in the paper. Have you heard that white people are starting to join, nice white Christian people." Splinters could stand no more. He looked directly at Lois and said, "Then nice white Christian people who voted for Richard Nixon are still 'lynching' nice negro Christian people." That remark got the whole table staring at him, with Lois smoldering with rage. At that point, Dad looked at his watch and said they had better be getting home soon.

After Boomer and Splinters arrived home, they immediately called Norm and Jon. There was suddenly a lead. Splinters read the article in The Columbus Evening Dispatch. It did mention the rise of the Ku Klux Klan, even in the moderately political Columbus metro area. It showed a picture of the "Grand Wizard" outside his head quarters on West Broad Street. Splinters looked closely at the picture, not believing if his eyes were seeing the picture right. He showed the picture to Boomer. Boomer gasped and whispered, "Oh my god, it's Inspector Scharffenberg"!

The next day was a holiday, so the four sleuths met in the basement at Norm's house. They were alone in the home when the doorbell rang. Norm ran up to answer the door, and he came down the basement steps with none other than Vincie! Vincie was attending South High School in Columbus now and living with the old woman who had taken him in years before, when he had run from his criminal guardians. The boys shook Vincie's hand and welcomed him. He also had read yesterday's paper, and he wanted to help the boys, however he could.

Norm began the meeting, saying he felt it wise to leave things alone until they had more information. "Inspector Scharffenberg must know what he is doing by becoming a part of the KKK. It is the smartest, although the riskiest, way to gather his information. Remember he is an infiltrator, a spy". Jon agreed, as did Splinters and Boomer. Vincie did volunteer to spy occasionally on the West Broad Street headquarters, and the matter was set for a vote. It seemed to be about the only thing to do right now. The vote was unanimous, as long as Vincie stayed a safe distance away.

Chapter Seven

For the next month Vincie performed surveillance on the KKK headquarters in west Columbus. He saw very little of consequence, other than a few of the same people coming and going. One person he identified was the inspector, usually wearing the outfit of a white class laborer with Levis, flannel shirts and a work coat. He drove an old Hudson Hornet. He looked inconspicuous. Vincie was excited at his sighting. He now knew the inspector was still with the organization. Vincie saw a few men, who wore business coats, suits and hats. One of them drove a new Lincoln Continental and was obviously wealthy; he dressed in a business suit and wool overcoat. He wished he could tail some of these men, however walking or taking the bus would be quite difficult. He could always heist a car, but he did not want to break the law. Vincie found a breakfast coffee shop-café nearby to spend his time. He knew he would also have to continue to not be identified. He dressed like an Ohio State student and always carried a few books with him, as if he were studying.

Christmas came to Worthington, bringing with it a mild snow. Splinters was hoping for more snow, a lot more snow, so the family did not have to drive to Don and Lois's home for

Christmas Eve. Twice in a month was more than he could partake of his aunt. Twice in twenty years was too often also, he thought and grinned. Luck was with him that day, when Lois called to cancel. Don, reportedly, had a very bad cold. Splinters felt maybe she did not want Splinters coming. After Thanksgiving she had told Mom that Splinters had not yet called her to apologize. Mom told her she had no idea what she was talking about. Lois told her that she had been terribly insulted by Splinters on Christmas Eve. Mom told her, "Oh that, he talks to me like that all the time". Hanging up the phone, Mom muttered, "That old bag". Splinters laughed.

The family reveled in their own private Christmas Eve. It felt cozy with the snow falling in the woods and the creek around them. Dad built a roaring fire in the stone fireplace that separated the living room from the kitchen. Mom made her wonderful chocolate cookies in the Kitchen-Aid oven, built into the stone. She also prepared hot cocoa.

They opened their presents at 7:00 PM. Splinters and Boomer received clothes, nothing but clothes. Then in a corner Splinters spied a large box that had not been there an hour ago. Dad picked it up and brought it to the center of the living room. The boys hastily opened it. It was an RCA covered record player that played 33, 45 and 78 rpm records. This one would replace their small RCA 45 rpm record player. Splinters could not wait to play it in their bedroom. Dad said to wait a minute, there was more. This was an incredible Christmas Eve! He gave them five rpm records each. He must have been looking in their record collection, as the boys had not collected any of the ten they had just received. Mom told them there was one condition. They had to play their records in the north half of the basement. They were not excited about that, until she shoved them down to the basement. It was still cement block walls, but Mom and Dad had filled the room with a sofa, chairs, table and floor lamps. Mom and Dad told the twins they wanted Norm and Jon over more frequently, so it was important the four teenage boys have a meeting room that was fun for them. She said she appreciated Norm's parents letting the boys use their family room, but she wanted Norm and Jon to feel comfortable to play their records and have their parties in their home also.

Splinters was so excited he called Jon to come over in the morning. Jon said he would call Norm. Instead of going to bed, they decided to set up their new record player in their new "basement family room". It was a cozy room as there was a nice off-white rug with the furniture surrounding it. The boys finished their work and began playing their new records. Splinters fell asleep on the sofa, and Boomer in the easy chair.

Boomer had received "Tossing And Turning" by Bobby Lewis; "Michael" by The Highwaymen; "Raindrops" by Dee Clark; "Hit

The Road Jack" by Ray Charles; Take Good Care Of My Baby" by Bobby Vee. Boomer said he got all records he had wanted.

Splinters had received "My True Story" by The Jive Five; "The Way You Look Tonight" by The Letterman(It reminded him of Sherry Perry and French kissing); "Daddy's Home by Shep and the Limelites; "Blue Moon" by The Marcels; "It's Gonna' Work Out Fine" by Ike And Tina Turner. They were all records he wanted, and, except for one, they were all rhythm 'n blues classics. Boomer must have told Mom and Dad what Splinters had wanted, as he had told Mom and Dad what Boomer had wanted. "Thanks, bud", Splinters told him. Boomer responded with "Thanks, bud". Their brother Bob had started the "bud" practice so the three brothers had all addressed each other alike.

Chapter Nine

Norm and Jon arrived around 10:00 am, after they had opened their presents. Jon had received clothes and speedo swimsuits, as he was still teaching swimming, now indoors. Norm had received a new Concord covered 45 rpm record player. Inside the player were twenty 45 rpm records. The boys were excited to now have thirty new 45's they could sing and dance to. Mom, first of all, brought cookies and milk down with her two Brenda Lee records. She put those two on the record player and danced with Jon to the first one, and with Norm to the second one. The boys partied in their new room the entire day. They even allowed Virginia Kay to come down for an hour. She and Jon danced the whole hour. Jon had no siblings and was so fond of Virginia Kay.

The snow increased in intensity and accumulation. Dad would not be able to drive Norm and Jon home as he did not have tire chains. The four boys decided to walk, wanting to get outside in the storm. The twins walked with Norm and Jon through the storm, laughing and playing in the snow. As Boomer and Splinters walked back home, a figure in a hooded woolen parka walked by them at New England Avenue and Morning Street. "Tell Vincie to stay away" was all he said! He continued walking down snowy Morning Street. It was Inspector Scharffenberg!

When the boys arrived home, Mom was talking to Grandaddy. She gave the phone to Splinters, so he could wish him a Merry Christmas. Grandaddy, rather, told him to heed the warning. Splinters knew what he meant.

Chapter Ten

January swept in windy and cold. It was back to school. Latin class was becoming more interesting with Mrs. Drumm. But one day she received a note that her mother had just passed away in Pennsylvania. Obviously distraught by the news, she ran around the classroom, muttering Latin phrases about Aeneas no one could understand. She said she feared for Dido! It was as if she were in her own world of The Aeneid. Finally, the principal, Mr. Andreas came into the classroom and led her away. Mrs. Drumm would be away for the next two months. She was replaced that day and the next two months by the ever-fearless Miss Frye. Miss Frye did not tolerate any humor in her classroom. She knew her Latin and expected each and every one of her students to know theirs. Splinters studied twice as hard, but he was learning so much English grammar from the Latin from this quite remarkable, if not sour, teacher.

Nineteen sixty-two brought with it incredible rock 'n roll. Norm always had money, and by March had collected his own top forty. By the end of the year, Splinters felt the best songs of 1962 to be: "I Can't Stop Loving You" by the great Ray Charles. He took a Don Gibson country song and made it into an aching rhythm 'n blues classic. Gene Chandler had a cape and was royalty when he sang “Duke Of Earl”. “Twist And Shout” by The Isley Brothers was fast and furious, a song years later The Beatles loved and recorded. “Wah Watusi” by The Orlons was also a great new hit and dance craze. But Norm also bought silly songs like “Rinky Dink” by Dave Baby Cortez, “A Little Bitty Tear” by Burl Ives, “Alley Cat” by Bent Fabric, and “Ahab the Arab” by Ray Stevens. There were two great songs, called the new Motown sound, “My Guy” and “You Beat Me to the Punch” by Mary Wells. Norm especially loved both of those songs. Rock ‘n roll enthusiasts were saying on TV that she was going to be the queen of rock ‘n roll. But it was not to be once Diana Ross started singing with The Supremes.

The four young men spent many evenings in one or the other basement family rooms listening to 45’s. They were amassing a large collection of music. They focused on school and their social life and tried to forget any bad thoughts, or fearful ones. These four young men just wanted to be normal teenage boys.

In March, there was grim news. Splinters was reading The Columbus Evening Dispatch and found an article about the disappearance of the Grand Wizard of the Columbus branch of the KKK. This was alarming and shocking, because this meant Inspector Scharffenberg was again missing. Did he leave on his own? Was his cover blown? Was he murdered? Splinters felt frightened and called Jon, while Boomer called Norm. Jon said he was heading over to the twins' home. Norm was not allowed out of his home due to a high fever and scratchy throat. There was no call from Grandaddy.

Jon arrived in his father's car. He had turned sixteen and now had his driver's license. He told Splinters his dad was going to give him his 1961 Plymouth Valiant, if Jon continued to receive good grades and stay on the swim team. Jon told Splinters he was back to dating Penny, now that he had a car. He told Splinters that Penny's friend, Candy Mc Manus liked Splinters. Jon had set up a double-date for the four of them the next weekend. Splinters liked Candy, but she was not beautiful like Joan or Sherry. But Jon convinced him they would have a great time. They were going to the Beechwold Theatre for a movie, then to Dave's Drive-In for a late supper.

Chapter Eleven

Jon and Penny picked up Splinters in the Valiant and drove to Candy's home in Colonial Hills. Splinters remarked to Jon he drove very carefully, and Jon said he was making sure his dad would give him that car in May. Candy was as fun as she always was. Splinters liked her because she was a nice girl, and she cracked a lot of jokes. They drove south on High Street to the theater. "Lawrence of Arabia" was a huge hit of a movie. All four of them sat in the "kissing" section, where all the teenagers sat. The adults knew never to sit in that section. Candy was to Splinter's left and Jon to his right. Jon and Penny began to French kiss, as soon as the lights dimmed. Splinters felt unsure what to do. He sat there with his hands in his lap. Finally, one quarter through the movie, Jon took Splinter's left hand and put it into Candy's lap. Candy reached down to take his hand in her lap and smiled right into Splinter's eyes. Jon just beamed. Splinters nudged him with his other elbow. Penny looked over and gave an approving smile.

About twenty minutes later Candy moved her face close to Splinters and kissed him on the neck. Splinters turned toward her, began kissing her, then he applied his best French technique. Her face felt warm. For the last half of the movie they continued kissing. Jon and Penny were kissing also, but Jon now had his big hands all over her body. This was heavy petting! Splinters was not prepared to go that far with Candy. They just kissed. Splinters felt Jon was a great deal more experienced with sex than he was. He knew the right spots of Penny's body to tenderly, and to eagerly, touch. Splinters felt inadequate for a couple reasons. Jon was a sex machine, and it aroused Splinters. Was he, Splinters, not skilled in lovemaking, or was he feeling physical attractions to Jon?

The meal at Dave's Drive-In was the usual-hamburgers, fries and a milkshake. Splinters became worried he might not have enough money for the bill, but Jon grabbed it and paid the bill. He must have sensed Splinter's worry. Jon was sensitive like that. Jon drove north on High Street toward Worthington, dropping Candy off first, and then Penny.

Jon then drove through town, telling Splinters he wanted to talk. As they drove through Worthington with the heater blasting and WCOL blasting the top 40, Jon told Splinters he was glad the two of them were friends. Jon said he had to confess something to Splinters. Splinters told him they were best friends, and he should tell him anything on his mind. Jon stopped the car and kept the heater at full blast. He told Splinters, when he saw Splinters kissing Candy, he wished Splinters had been kissing him instead. Splinters smiled at him and told him he felt honored that such a good looking guy like Jon liked him. Jon told Splinters he definitively liked him, but more than that, he was beginning to fall in love with him. Splinters felt embarrassed, but he also felt somewhat aroused. Jon leaned over Splinters, hugging and kissing him, and finally kissing him on the lips. Splinters felt a warmth from Jon he had never felt before, not to mention the warmth he felt in his loins. He did not tell Jon he felt he could never be attracted to other boys. Rather, Splinters stammered a bit and said, "Jon, I like you a lot, as my friend, but I don't think I should be attracted to another boy". It wasn't wrong, it just wasn't him, or was it? Splinters told him Mom, Dad, Ree and Boomer would not like him being "that different". But at the same time, Splinters was wondering if he felt the same as Jon did for him. He was physically aroused, as was Jon. He thought about the day at the Worthington pool, when Jon had first smiled at him. Splinters had felt back then excitement, if not arousal. Now Jon knew Splinters was aroused, but being the gentleman he was, Jon told Splinters they would continue to act "normal", because their families would not understand. But between the two of them there could be love, spiritual love. He added it might grow to a deeper love. Splinters agreed. It was difficult for him to say he agreed, but he knew deep inside he also loved this wonderful and handsome man. Jon then held his whole body close to Splinters. Splinters joked that he was getting very hot and perhaps Jon should turn down the heater. Jon laughingly asked, "which heater?", and then responded with his full distinctive laugh switching off the heat, from the car heater. However Jon's heat continued to radiate. Splinters then did the unexpected. He grabbed Jon around the neck and hugged him as tight as he could, "I do love you, you big homo". Splinters was happily crushed by Jon's hot athletic body, as Jon tightly hugged him.

Both boys laughed as Jon drove to Splinter's home with a big smile on his face. Splinters was relieved about their talk and physical encounter, but he had such conflicted feelings. When he fell asleep that night he thought of Jon as the friend he would probably never again have in his lifetime. Jon was one of a kind. Splinters knew Jon would always be there for him and he knew he would think have a place in his heart for Jon long after their teenage years.

Chapter Twelve

Summer and the end of school arrived. Splinters could not believe he was halfway through high school already. He and Boomer had both decided they would try out for the cross country team in the fall, in eleventh grade, as they had both been on the track team the spring of 1962 and had run well at the mile. They might even do better running two miles. Coach Eisenhart had encouraged them to try-out, adding if they ‘got the lead out of their asses”, he was sure they could earn “letters” in cross country.

The twins now had their own car. They had passed the driver test in May, although it took Splinters three times to pass parallel parking in Dad’s 1960 Mercury. Dad had found them an exotic car. Mr. Snouffer had garaged his 1947 Chrysler Town and Country four door, with real wood on the sides, trunk and luggage rack. He kept it garaged for two years and told Dad it would be perfect for the twin’s first car. Dad bought if from the kind old man for $15. Splinters loved the car when he first saw it. But driving it was a chore! It was a mammoth car, but it did have an grand old style. The boys kept it until school started, but they felt other students would laugh at the car, if they drove it to school. It was more of an old woman’s car, not for a teenager. In fall of 1962 they traded it for a 1953 red Studebaker Champion. That car had European styling and had been designed by Raymond Loewy and was known as the "Loewy Coupe". It was a classic. Splinters loved the car, but Boomer told him Stupid-Bakers had a bad reputation of rusting out easily and using a great deal of oil. Both were true as rust spots started appearing in a few months, and the car needed a change of oil with every refill of gas.

There had been no word from Inspector Scharffenberg, and it was possible he had been kidnapped or murdered by the KKK. Then one day the phone rang. Splinters answered it, and it was Vincie. He told Splinters the four boys had to meet at Bernies the next morning, to talk. He had confidential information, so it was essential the four of them be there at ten am. Splinters saw Jon lifeguarding at the pool that day. He was teaching morning swim classes but could get away for one morning. Norm was not working and said he would be there at ten. Norm was now driving an Oldsmobile F-85, a cute compact car his parents had bought for him.

The Valiant, Chrysler and Oldsmobile parked on High Street. Jon, as usual, opened the doors of the drug store for the three others. He smiled at Splinters, as he was heading in front of Jon. Jon came up to him, putting his arms around Splinter's shoulders and told him he had missed him lately. Splinters told him he felt the same, and Jon gave him, what he told Splinters was a "love punch".

Vincie was already seated with four extra phosphates, two cherrys and two limes. As Splinters sucked in the delicious cherry, Vincie began talking. He told the guys that the inspector was still alive, and that he had been helping him on "surveillance matters". Inspector Scharffenberg had made several trips to America's deep South to meet "Grand Dragons". He was now a trusted member in the KKK, but the four boys must not say a word to anyone, including Grandaddy. It was too dangerous. The inspector had been gathering information on violent acts the KKK members had committed in the American south. The inspector was working closely with the FBI to bring charges against several members for murder and violent assaults on black people and white civil rights workers.

Then Vincie told them they had an assignment. The inspector suspected a school teacher at Worthington High School of violence against a Negro family in Alabama. He had been a new teacher in Worthington in the fall of 1961, having moved from a small Alabama town. He was a history teacher, named Mr. Kibbons, and he already had a poor reputation with the other teachers, the administration and most of his students due to his ignoring black students in his class. Mr. Kibbons seemed to feel himself superior to negroes. Splinters had never had him as a teacher, but he already felt he would not like him. However, Mr. Kibbons would continue teaching in the fall of 1962, as Mr. Andreas had approved him for another year. (He had been asked to do so by the FBI, but none of the students knew that news). Vincie told the boys that all four of them would be his pupils, when school began in the fall. They were only to pay attention for any suspicious activity, but they could not put themselves in danger. They were also instructed to join "The History Club", as Mr. Kibbons headed it. The club would meet weekly after school, once school began. It would take place on Fridays only, because Norm and Jon had swimming practice (Norm was a manager), and Splinters and Boomer had cross country practice.

Vincie said he had to leave the meeting, as he started to get up. Jon had to get back to swimming lessons and lifeguard duty. Norm and the twins walked back to Norm's house. They talked again about how they were now in danger for a second time, and these people were very ruthless and evil. They would only gather information.

Chapter Thirteen

The summer turned out to be a typical central Ohio season, hot and humid. Splinters and Boomer rode their bikes to the pool, rather than drive their "wooden Chrysler". It consumed a lot of gas, and they were still only working on weekends cleaning offices.

Jon continued his lifeguard job at the pool. Norm met the twins weekly at the pool. They listened to the summer songs of 1962 on the outdoor juke box at pool-side. Splinter's liked the new group, The Beach Boys. "Surfin' USA" was fun to sing to and dance to. Jon knew Splinters liked it, and he often walked over to play it, giving Splinters and the group his big smile. One day Candy was with them and asked the others if they thought Jon might be a homo. Splinters told her he was sure he was not. "Well, he sure seems to like you", she replied. Boomer asked her if she would not like Jon if he were a homo. She instantly replied, "I'd love that hunk of a man, whatever he is". The whole group laughed. Splinters smiled and silently agreed.

Splinters loved a new song by a relatively unknown group named, The Crystals. Their song was a girl song about a girl being in love with a boy from another part of town who comes

“Uptown” to see her. It was about love with a guy who was “different”. Splinters wondered just what “different” meant. When Splinters talked privately to Jon about the song and guys who were “different”, Jon said he was different. Splinters said he was beginning to feel that way also, as Jon had aroused some “different” feelings in him. “Now you know how I have felt about you ever since I first met you”, Jon replied. He held Splinter’s face in his warm hands and kissed him deeply. Splinters knew he was loving this attention, coming from a friend he loved this deeply. Splinters was loving it. They kissed and hugged for the next two hours in Jon’s bedroom, listening to Jon’s 45’s. Afterwards, once Splinters arrived home, he felt guilty about having been kissing his male friend. He wanted to tell Mom about his feelings, but she might think him too “different” and have a hard time accepting his actions. He was fearful she might also take him to see a psychiatrist or tell Dad about what he had done. He could not begin to even think that his parents might banish Jon from their home and from their son because Jon was “different”.

Dance songs became very popular that summer and everyone was moving to the beats and melodies. In Splinter’s case it was more like trying to dance to them successfully. He did not feel he had the “beat” and the right form for these dances. The Watusi was popular. The Mashed Potato dance was also popular with Dee Dee Sharpe singing “The Mashed Potato

Time" and "Gravy (For My Mashed Potatoes)". The Twist was still popular: "Twist Twist Senora" and "Dear Lady Twist" by Gary US Bonds; "Soul Twist" by King Curtis; "The Twist" (third year in a row on the charts) and "Slow Twistin' by Chubby Checker; "Twistin' the Night Away" by Sam Cooke; "Twist and Shout" by The Isley Brothers; "Twistin' Matilda" by Jimmy Soul; "Percolator Twist" by Billy Joe And The Checkmates. Splinters loved a great slow song by Barbara Lynn, "You'll Lose a Good Thing". It was unusual, because it combined rock with some blues and jazz.

The summer was a good one, and it ended on a fun note. Mom and Dad rented their usual cottage on Indian Lake, and rented a boat, using Dad's Evinrude outboard motor. Dad preferred Evinrude to Johnson. They both seemed the same to Splinters. Norm and Jon drove to the lake to stay for a few days. They slept in the living room of the three bedroom lakeside cottage. Dad always had the boat out in the mornings, and he let the boys use it in the afternoons. They took the boat each day to Hermit Island to swim at the beach, and took it to both amusement parks. They drove to miniature golf. They had such fun and forgot about the drama back home.

August turned to September. Now it was Miss Frye to teach Latin for the full year, and she was still a very strict and sour teacher. It was now Mr. Kenneth Kibbons teaching American

History. It was now Mr. Kibbons monitoring and mentoring the history club. It was time for more investigations.

Chapter Fourteen

The four friends decided to enter history class separately and to sit away from each other, so as to not attract attention to their close friendship. The first day of class was their introduction to a man who could be a possible criminal and a violent person. They had to be careful. All of their meetings took place in one of the two basement family rooms, never at Bernies anymore. Danger was felt by all four of them.

Mr. Kibbons appeared on the surface to be a highly intelligent and friendly teacher. He respected students who expressed an interest in history. It was obvious he also expected to have his respect reciprocated. Splinters thought he was an excellent teacher. His active teaching style made American history interesting, and he seemed to express no biases or prejudices. He discussed the Civil War and its' aftermath very objectively. Splinters felt he was going to be a "tough nut to crack". He also knew this was not a teacher to feel any closeness to, but rather he would show respect to Mr. Kibbons.

The history club was comprised of only ten students, but the other six students knew the four boys only from past classes together. There were no other close friends in class. Mr. Kibbons was an excellent leader. As the fall turned to winter, the four boys met and began to see some favoritism on Mr.

Kibbon's part. Jon was beginning to be one of his favorites. In the family room discussions, Norm pointed out that Jon had the "all American look" and a great deal of respect for older authority figures. Norm felt he was one of Kibbon's least favorites. Norm was not the all American boy in his looks. Norm admitted he was also a smart aleck toward other students and toward older authority figures. Mr. Kibbons liked both Boomer and Splinters for their physical looks (they had a definite English look), but he seemed to perceive their lack of respect for authority figures. Norm told the other three Jon was their best bet to get close to Mr. Kibbons. However, there was another student Mr. Kibbons obviously liked even more than Jon.

The other student was a boy name Peter Harrington. Peter was from a prosperous family, who had moved to Worthington four years ago from Atlanta, Georgia. Peter was intellectually gifted , and an honor student at Worthington High School. His father owned a successful business west of Columbus, and his mother was involved in a successful downtown business. Peter was well respected by students, staff and teachers. He quickly became President of the history club. It was apparent Mr. Kibbons had chosen him over Jon.

Peter was a handsome teenager with blonde hair, blue eyes and brilliant white teeth that could match Jon's perfect smile. He dressed in white or blue button-down oxford shirts. He was immaculately dressed in pressed Levis or khaki pants and polished cordovan penny loafers. Splinters thought they looked like his "Weejuns", but Boomer said Peter's shoes were probably "Bostonians". Peter was always polite to students and teachers. He was also polite to the four boys, but he seemed to especially like Jon.

Peter's academic skills were excellent, and he always volunteered for projects. He also had good ideas in history club, although Jon's ideas appeared more creative and daring. One of Jon's ideas was to explore and gather research on the Ku Klux Klan. Mr. Kibbons, initially did not approve of his idea, but he agreed once he saw that Peter was in full agreement of the idea. Peter was a boy who was open to other's ideas.

Thus, the history club took on the history of the Ku Klux Klan as their research subject.

Chapter Fifteen

Peter Harrington lived with his parents in Medick Estates in a life of luxury. The home was a mansion from the 1920's. Splinters heard that it had eight bedrooms and ten bathrooms. His father drove a 1961 Lincoln Continental, and his mother drove a stunning 1960 Lincoln Premiere. It seemed to Splinters that Peter did care about people who were middle class rather than rich, and he never seemed to have prejudices against any of the minority students. He seemed perfect. "Too perfect", Splinters thought. He might not show his prejudices, but he also had no black friends, no minority friends of any kind.

Jon became friends with Peter, and that friendship seemed to be blossoming into a genuine one. Jon also kept his close friendship with Boomer, Splinters and Norm. But Jon and Peter were invited to Mr. Kibbbons' home for lunch and discussions on topics such as the civil rights movement. Jon told the other boys that he thought at first the teacher was a champion for the rights of minorities. But as the discussions progressed, it became obvious he was politically to the far right. He told Peter and Jon he was an avid member of The John Birch Society, an organization Splinters knew believed in segregation of the races. Jon later told Splinters that organization was to the right of Louis XIV!

Jon, Norm, Boomer and Splinters continued their own discussions in Norm's or the twin's basement. Vincie also started to attend the secret meetings. Mom thought the five boys were listening to rock 'n roll, but they were secretly considering their next moves. Jon told the others he did not want to put Peter in any danger. The other boys agreed. It was also agreed that Vincie would begin surveillance on Mr. Kibbons, his whereabouts and his comings and goings. Vincie had bought a 1953 Desoto the past summer and could now follow the teacher. Jon would keep an eye on him during the meetings with the teacher and Peter. Mr. Kibbons lived just north of Ohio State University campus, in the Clintonville area of Columbus.

Once they had all arrived, Jon said he had something of value to report to the other boys. As they listened to rock 'n roll in Norm's basement, the five of them listened to Jon's discovery. One day after Mr. Kibbons had taken Peter outside for a walk, Jon had decided instead to read a book in his study. As the other two walked, Jon went carefully through some papers on Mr. Kibbon's desk. At first they all appeared to be school papers, but underneath that stack, Jon found a manila folder that displayed "Project Dark Storm" on the index tab. Jon began to read it. It described a project that would be starting in early 1963 to rid the South of "freedom riders", civil right activists , and other troublemakers from the North. It was a terrorist plot to place bombs in luggage on the buses to be detonated, once the riders had boarded the buses. Jon quickly put the folder back and stacked the papers on it, before Peter and Mr. Kibbons returned from their walk. When they finally did walk into the study, Jon was busy reading.

The five boys in the basement, hearing this shocking news from Jon, decided they needed a plan. First, Vincie would relay this news to Inspector Scharffenberg. Vincie would follow the teacher every night, to find out where he was meeting his fellow co-conspirators. Jon had done a great job, but Norm suggested Jon lay off his meetings with Mr. Kibbons over the holiday season. The other four agreed. It was becoming too dangerous for Jon. Jon said he would like to continue his friendship with Peter, so as not to arouse any attention or suspicion to himself. Everyone agreed each one of them must very careful, and very cautious.

Jon and Peter became close friends. And then Peter told Jon something. It was a week before Christmas, when Jon visited Peter at his home. Jon felt shock when Peter asked Jon to join a particular organization. As soon as Jon arrived home from Peter's home he called Splinters. He told him he had some shocking news. A meeting was arranged that evening at Norm's house. Vincie was not present, because he was tailing Mr. Kibbons.

Jon told the three boys that Peter had told Jon he was also a member of "The John Birch Society", and he wanted Jon to join. Peter's parents had been longstanding members of the society. Jon told Peter he would have to do some research about becoming a member, but he knew what his decision would be. Peter told him the society was an exclusive club to keep America strong in electing political officials who were determined to maintain the "white status quo". Jon knew the "John Birch Society" was a bit more than simply maintaining the status quo. It represented ultra far-right causes. Jon thought the members were similar to the Nazis under Adolf Hitler.

The four boys told Jon he had handled the talk with Peter well. They all felt Jon should continue his contact and friendship with Peter. Norm pointed out that an ultra-conservative group like The John Birchers was not necessarily a violent group like the Ku Klux Klan. Jon totally disagreed, and he told Norm it probably instructed others to perform the violent deeds. Splinters told the group he felt they were getting in way over their heads. They had reported Jon's discovery of the conspiracy in Mr. Kibbon's study to the inspector, but perhaps, they needed to stay out of the whole mess. "Who knows what Peter's parents are like? They could be as bad as Vincie's so-called parents had been", he said. Splinters also pointed out these people had a great deal of money and probably had a great deal of power. Peter's father's Lincoln had also been seen near the KKK headquarters. Splinters directly told Jon he feared for his safety. Jon smiled at his dear friend and took his arm in his.

After the meeting Jon told Splinters he needed some time with Splinters, together and alone. He knew Splinters was the one friend in whom he could completely confide, and who understood Jon's feelings. Splinters suggested they have a good time together that night and drive to see a movie-and not talk about any of the dramatic events that were unfolding. Jon said, "It's my treat, and I'm driving". Splinters was excited to have a night alone with Jon.

Chapter Sixteen

That night Jon drove with Splinters to the Clintonville Theater to watch, “To Kill A Mockingbird”. Jon was tearful during some of the scenes, especially the courtroom part and the violent murder of the black man on trial. Splinters cried also. Jon looked at him and whispered, “Aren’t we being babies”. He then took Splinter’s hand and held it tight to the end of the movie, and Splinters held that warm hand right back as tight as he could. After the movie they sat in the theater for ten minutes, discussing how unfair segregation had always been in the country. They agreed they had to continue pursuing their investigation and hoped they could do some good for oppressed people and for the sake of their country.

Leaving the theater, Jon told Splinters he had decided they were going to an all night coffee shop close to campus, which was a “beatnik” hangout. There, he said, they could talk and just have a mellow night together. Splinters agreed. They drove to “The Sacred Mushroom” and listened to folk music, which was beginning to become popular on the American music scene. Jon had come up with a wonderful idea. Splinters loved the atmosphere. He told Jon he bet a lot of the beatniks smoked marijuana. Jon said he was sure they did. They sat close together, drinking delicious coffee and watching the scene before them. They listened to Joan Baez, The Kingston Trio, and Pete Seeger. They sang along to The Rooftop Singers recording of "Walk Right In". They listened to poetry readings. Splinters was feeling so comfortable with the whole atmosphere and with Jon, he told Jon he wished they had a "reefer" to smoke. Jon laughed and told Splinters, if they had smoked a reefer, he would be dong more than holding his hand. They both laughed and Jon held Splinter's hand even tighter.

As they drove home, Splinters told Jon they would be friends forever. Jon replied that he hoped so, but that once high school was over, they might take different paths. Jon told Splinters he was not sure he wanted to attend Ohio State University. He said he might join the US Marines. His frank reply startled Splinters. He could not think of life without Jon. Splinters told Jon that this night they would sleep together. Splinters said he just wanted to hold Jon all night in Jon's bed. That night, in their underwear and t-shirts they kissed and held one another, as if they would never see each other again. Splinters insisted on keeping on some clothes, as he could not sleep naked with anyone, not even Jon. Splinters had trouble getting to sleep, thinking his life would never be the same without this wonderful guy. It would change drastically after graduation. He knew Norm might separate from the twins, seeing how he was planning to work fulltime. But Splinters just could not conceive that Jon would separate from him. Jon had become the most valued friend Splinters had ever had. He was fearful, however, of losing Jon's friendship, once Jon joined the US Marines. He did not want to think Jon could ever be placed in any danger, like a war. He thought about how President Kennedy was increasing troops in the Republic of South Vietnam. He felt scared for Jon. He also felt a deep sense of love for him he could not explain. He moved as close to Jon as he could, thinking how warm and wonderful he felt with him. Jon, in a sleepy state, turned his head toward Splinters and said "I will always love you". Then they both cried, kissed deeply, and tasted each other's falling tears. The emotions were still so confusing to Splinters. It was definitely love, but it was also the fear of losing that love.

Chapter Seventeen

Back to school in January of 1963, in a year that would be like no other. Jon began to plan to gear-down his friendship with Peter. Jon, of course, had declined the offer to join The John Birch Society. Peter would now think of their friendship differently because Jon said "no" to him. How could Jon get any help from Peter, now that Jon had rebuffed Peter's offer? He felt he was a chess piece in a larger and very scary game, and he hoped he had made the right move. He was unsure as to how to proceed with Peter.

Peter was not accepting Jon's refusal to join, so Peter continued his pitch. He told Jon that he and his family had other societies, with which they had close contacts. These societies could benefit John as far as power and great wealth. These organizations carried out the orders from societies like The John Birch Society, in order to maintain the "status quo". Jon felt what Peter was telling him was garbage, however he might gather some useful information from Peter. He told Jon he needed a messenger, one who would carry out Peter's orders. Jon spontaneously burst out laughing at Peter's words. He joked that it sounded like a bunch of clowns giving and taking orders, and he said, "You are such a good friend but such a clown". Peter was insulted, and his reaction was chilly toward

Jon. Had Jon, due to his spontaneity and firm values, lost Peter forever. John felt very stressed and knew he had gotten way over his head into something vile and evil.

Later that day Jon called Vincie to give him a code word, "beatnik", which meant he had information for Inspector Scharffenberg and they had to meet. Vincie would forward all information to the inspector. The meeting place had already been agreed on. It was certainly not Bernie's. It was in the Lazarus Downtown Department Store, women's lingerie. There Jon gave Vincie the information. He told him it might be the KKK following orders of Peter and his father. Jon felt it to be a distinct possibility. Vincie said he would immediately meet with the inspector, and he told Jon to be extra cautious about any other contacts with Peter. Jon agreed, and they parted.

By early February no other information was given to Jon by Peter. However, the news broke on February 27th that three Ku Klux Klan organizations had been raided by FBI agents. They were being closed due to possible charges of attempted murder of "Freedom Riders". One was the KKK in Columbus. Another was in Atlanta. Another was in a small Mississippi town. Peter had disappeared, along with his parents. Mr. Kibbons had been arrested and was in federal custody. So far, there was no further information. The four boys had not heard from Vincie or from Inspector Scharffenberg. But they knew the message had been delivered!

The boys were initially happy and relieved that their work was over, that what they had reported was reported to the FBI, and they went into action. Jon told the twins "Sometimes justice is done".

That night the four boys celebrated in the Sielisch's basement. They were uncomfortable that the Harrington family had not been apprehended, but it was felt by all four the good guys did win, and it was only a matter of time until they would be caught. Late that night Norm and Boomer "crashed" in Norm's room. As they slept Jon and Splinters held hands and talked quietly. Splinters accepted Jon's invitation to sleep with him, across the street, in Jon's home and in Jon's bed. It was a night they never forgot. They felt each other to finally be together with no more stress and drama from sleuthing. They could now enjoy one another like they never had before.

Chapter Eighteen

Early that morning as Jon and Splinters were fast asleep, the phone rang. Jon had an extension phone in his room and quickly answered before his parents awoke to the ring.

It was Peter. He was drunk and telling Jon the most idiotic things. Jon seriously thought he was being a nut case. He told Jon his father had so much power, he could never get caught. Peter would succeed his father in his far right organizations, and Jon could become his assistant. He pleaded with Jon to join his cause. Then he told Jon the most chilling thing. He was rambling, and slurred his words. But Jon heard him say, "That Democrat Kennedy will get his, in the fall". Jon was numbed by what he was saying. Then he said something even much more odious, "Gun shot to the head in Texas", he cackled. Peter's demented laughter sounded cruel and insane. As Jon heard it could barely believe what he was hearing and put his finger over his mouth to alert the awakening Splinters to remain completely quiet. Jon then started laughing, saying, "Peter, you old drunk, get to bed. I can't understand a word you said". Jon froze for a minute, not knowing why he had reacted like that and was unsure of what to do next. He shook his head, and felt so powerless. Peter continued to laugh, to rant and to rave, at times screaming into the phone. Jon finally disconnected the phone.

Jon immediately started sobbing and looking at Splinters for help. Splinters had no idea what had just happened or what Jon had heard. In an almost hysterical sobbing voice, Jon related to Splinters what he had heard from Peter. Splinters gasped, and he was dumbfounded. "What should we do? We have to do something!", Splinters cried out. He held tightly onto Jon. Once Jon was a bit more composed, he told Splinters they had to find Vincie to tell him what had just happened and what he had just heard.

Jon called the only number he had. It was three am in the morning, and he was afraid no one would answer the phone. But, thank god, the old woman Vincie lived with answered the phone. Jon immediately apologized for disturbing her, but he told her who he was and that he had to talk to Vincie immediately. It was an emergency! Two minutes later Vincie was on the phone. "Beatnik, now" Jon cried out to his friend. Vincie responded to Jon he would meet him in their alternative meeting place, by Schmidts Sausage Haus, in German Village.

Splinters and Jon quietly left the bedroom and the Cagan home, feeling lucky that Jon's parents had not awakened to the solitary ring of the phone when Peter had called. They ran to the Valiant, and Jon drove with speed, but not carelessness down High Street toward German Village. Splinters and Jon were too shocked still to talk, so they remained pretty much silent. Splinters seemed to calm Jon by holding onto his arm as Jon drove. There was no music from the radio. How could they listen to their rock 'n roll at a time like this?

It took a half hour to reach Schmidt's, and Vincie's Desoto was parked in the parking lot as they arrived. Jon told Vincie as calmly as he could what he had heard from Peter. It took Vincie several minutes to absorb what Jon had just told him. Vincie's first reaction to the news was that if he reported what he had just heard, the inspector and his higher authorities would think he and Jon were "nutcases". "Vincie, you have to report it. It may not yet be a crime, but if it is true and it happens, it will be the worst American tragedy since Pearl Harbor". Vincie did finally agree with Jon and said he would contact the inspector right away. Vincie, in a pleading voice, told Jon and Splinters to not contact him again. He would get back to them, once he knew the authorities, mainly the FBI, had the information from Inspector Scharffenberg. Vincie ran to his car and sped west toward downtown Columbus.

Jon and Splinters drove back to Worthington, again holding on to one another but saying nothing but, "Oh my god, this is a horrible nightmare". Jon dropped Splinters at his home, and Jon returned to his home.

Jon immediately fell asleep, but he woke at ten am to the phone ringing. His parents must be at work, he thought. He answered the phone. It was Peter! "Oh good, I got hold of you! Did I call you late last night or early this morning? Did I say anything?" Jon laughed and said: "Yeah, you did call me, but you just sputtered drunken gibberish. I could not understand a word you said." Jon could feel his heart beating. Peter at once sounded relieved, believing what Jon had just told him."Get back to bed, old friend. Sorry I called you". Peter then hung up. Jon felt relieved, but Peter's earlier rantings and prophecy stayed in his head. "Could it be true? How could something so evil like that happen? Had he done everything he could do to stop it, if it was real? Would he and Splinters ever be the same, after they had to share such a monstrous secret?

Chapter Nineteen

February turned into March. No word from anyone. No word from Vincie. No word from Inspector Scharffenberg. April turned into the summer, then into early fall. In October, Jon was a senior in high school and was again on the swim team. The twins were doing well in cross country and would receive "letters". He and Splinters met occasionally, but they did not know what to say to one another. They did not hold each other. They did not talk about what had happened that night. They were waiting for news. They had become disconnected. Splinters tried to be positive toward Jon, telling him that the incident would have been handled in a covert manner to protect national security and the presidency of the United States. They might not hear anything. Jon said he did not feel good about their not hearing from anyone, especially the inspector and Vincie. He could not get hold of either one of them. Vincie had moved out of the south Columbus home the same day he had received the information from Jon. The old woman had not heard from him. As far as the inspector, even Grandaddy could not get hold of him or find out where he was.

They decided to wait. They would always regret that decision.

On November 22 1963, President John F. Kennedy was shot in the head and murdered in Dallas, Texas. They cried. The country was torn apart. Nothing had been done to prevent it. His terrible death tore apart the country. Splinter's idealism was gone. It changed Jon and Splinter's close friendship. They had a terrible time even talking to each other or meeting without feeling profound guilt and grief. They could not wipe the president's death from their brains. Their guilt was so profound due to no one, including themselves, stopping the horrendous crime. Neither one of them could shake their grief, their anguish.

Afterword

It was as if there was nothing more to say. Jon and Splinters drifted apart. They no longer talked to each other of the terror that had happened in November, or about what they knew. When they saw one another, each wanted to reach out to the other. It was in their faces when they saw each other, but the thoughts of the horror they knew stopped them. Neither one could do it. They could not admit their prior knowledge, even to themselves.

Jon escaped into the Marines in June of 1964. In 1965 Jon died thousands of miles away in an unknown base, called Chu Lai, in Quang Nai province. His cause of death was never known by anyone outside the immediate family, and Jon's parents carried their grief privately. Splinters felt such loss but could not explain that loss to any family member. Splinters lived with his deep loss and never told a soul anything, not even the eternal emptiness of losing his wonderful friend and partner

Splinters began attending classes at Ohio State University in September of 1964. He had thought about his love for Jon almost every day, after Jon had entered the military. After his death, Splinters would choke up even thinking of Jon. He dreamed about Jon, and he could sometimes smell Jon's musky masculinity, feel his warm hands and body, and hear his hearty peal of laughter. Then he went to Vietnam in 1969, having been drafted after graduation. It was an unfortunate place to live for fourteen months. It was Quang Ngai Province, the air base in Chu Lai. He felt for those fourteen months that four years ago Jon had once walked in this same place. He lived through it, but he could not ever get over the President's assassination and the close friendship and relationship he had once had with a wonderful guy named Jon.

What should have made them closer had only torn them further apart. It was loss. It was grief. It was guilt. Splinters would bear it all for his entire life. He told no one. How could he? In time he came to accept the tragedy that had befallen him and Jon, and the young president of the United States.